NIGHTMARE MAN

Tim Collins

Illustrated by Abby Ryder

HORROR HOTEL

Titles in Horror Hotel:

NIGHTMARE MAN
TIM COLLINS & ABBY RYDER

WALL CRAWLERS
TIM COLLINS & JAMES LAWRENCE

BED BUGS
TIM COLLINS & JAMES LAWRENCE

THE MIRROR
TIM COLLINS & JAMES LAWRENCE

THE LIFT
TIM COLLINS & ABBY RYDER

THIEF
TIM COLLINS & ABBY RYDER

Badger Publishing Limited, Oldmedow Road,
Hardwick Industrial Estate, King's Lynn PE30 4JJ

Telephone: 01438 791037
www.badgerlearning.co.uk

Nightmare Man ISBN 978-1-78837-417-0

2 4 6 8 10 9 7 5 3 1

NIGHTMARE MAN

Tim Collins
Illustrated by Abby Ryder

Contents

Badger
LEARNING

Story Vocabulary

thumping

staring

moaning

The story so far...

Jayden was on a walking holiday, but he had got lost and it was raining.

He came to an old hotel.

A woman stood at the door of the hotel.

"Welcome to Horror Hotel," she said. "I am the Manager. I hope you enjoy your stay with us."

Jayden didn't really want to stay in this strange hotel, but he knew it would only be for one night.

What could possibly go wrong? he thought.

Chapter 1

The Thin Man

A very tall, thin man was walking towards Jayden.

His long, sharp nails were dripping with blood.

He was getting closer and closer.

I must get back to my room, thought Jayden.

Jayden tried to run but his feet wouldn't move.

He was frozen with fear.

The man was getting nearer.

His sharp nails began to claw at
Jayden's arm.

Jayden's heart was thumping.

The man had six eyes.

Jayden heard someone screaming.

The screaming went on and on.

Then Jayden worked it out.

He was the one who was screaming.

Chapter 2

Awake

Jayden opened his eyes.

He had been dreaming.

He was in his bed in the strange hotel.

His heart was still thumping.

Jayden got up and sat on the edge of the bed.

The Manager came on the TV screen.

"What is the matter?" she asked. "Why were you screaming?"

"I had a nightmare," said Jayden.

"Sorry you had a nightmare," said the Manager. "I will play some music to help you get back to sleep."

"Thanks," said Jayden.

The TV screen went blank.

Then Jayden heard some music playing.

The music was like someone moaning.

Now I'll never get back to sleep, thought Jayden.

Jayden went to the bathroom.

He switched on the light.

The thin man from his nightmare was standing there.

His six eyes were staring at Jayden.

Chapter 3

Attack

The Nightmare Man's sharp nails tried to claw Jayden's face.

Jayden shut his eyes.

This is still a dream, he thought. *I woke up last time, and I'll wake up again.*

Jayden opened his eyes.

The Nightmare Man was still there.

When I wake up, thought Jayden, *I'm going to run until I'm miles away from this evil hotel.*

The Nightmare Man dug his nails deep into Jayden's face.

Jayden could feel blood dripping down his cheeks.

Jayden looked in the mirror.

Something had changed about his face.

Now he had six eyes like the Nightmare Man.

"Noooooo!" screamed Jayden.

Jayden tried to fight the Nightmare Man but he was too weak.

He sank to the floor and all the eyes on his face closed.

This time he didn't wake up.

Questions

Chapter 1

What does Jayden try and do when he sees the man? *(page 8)*

How many pairs of eyes had the man? *(page 10)*

Chapter 2

What does the Manager do to help Jayden get back to sleep? *(page 16)*

Does it work? *(page 19)*

Chapter 3

What does Jayden think when he sees the Nightmare Man? *(page 22)*

What does the Nightmare Man do to Jayden? *(page 28)*

About the Author

Tim Collins has written over 90 books for adults and children.

He enjoys reading horror books and playing computer games.

He's stayed in lots of scary hotels, but none of them were haunted as far as he knows.

About the Illustrator

Abby Ryder is a cartoonist who loves comic books and video games.

She thinks she is brave enough to spend a night at the Horror Hotel.